KU-033-445

© 1993 Geddes & Grosset Ltd
Published by Geddes & Grosset Ltd,
New Lanark, Scotland.

ISBN  1 85534 595 1

Printed and bound in Italy.

# The Fox and the Stork

Retold by Judy Hamilton
Illustrated by Lindsay Duff

**Tarantula Books**

The animals' Midsummer Ball was a great occasion. All the animals and birds forgot about their troubles for a while, forgave their enemies, made friends with strangers and gave themselves up to fun and merry-making. There was a feast of every kind of fancy food and drink and there was wonderful music playing all the time. In the warm midsummer air, throughout the long evening and the short starlit hours of night, the animals would dance until the sun began to rise again.

At one such Ball, the stork caught a glimpse of the handsome fox. She could not help staring at him, for he was looking particularly smart, his fine red fur shining with health, his dark eyes bright and intelligent.

Finally, she managed to catch his attention and was delighted when he asked her to dance. The fox was fun to dance with, for he was quick and light on his feet. The stork and the fox enjoyed several dances together, whirling and twirling and laughing as the music swept them along.

Just as dawn was about to break, they stopped for a moment to have a cooling drink.

The fox cleared his throat carefully and turned to the stork.

"Would you give me the pleasure of having dinner with me next week?" he asked.

The stork flushed with delight. "Thank you, Mr Stork. I would love to have dinner with you."

The stork took her time getting ready for her dinner date with the fox. She preened her feathers one by one, slowly and carefully, and rubbed her beak on them as she did so to give it a polish. She looked at herself in the mirror from every angle to make sure that not a feather was out of place. After one final check to make sure that she was looking her very best, she set off at last for the fox's house.

The stork arrived at the fox's house at exactly the right time, and rang the bell. Right away, the fox opened the door with a welcoming smile.

"Miss Stork! I'm so glad you could come! I must say you are looking very pretty tonight! Come in and make yourself at home."

The fox and the stork sat together talking comfortably for a while, remembering the fun that they had had at the Midsummer Ball and catching up on news.

"What a gentleman Mr Fox is," thought the stork, "and such pleasant company. I wonder what he has made me for dinner?"

The fox, as if reading the stork's mind, left the room and returned with two steaming plates.

"I do hope you are hungry, Miss Stork," he said. "I have made special soup. I hope you will like it!"

"I am sure that I will," the stork assured him. "It smells quite delicious!"

And as the fox laid the plates down on the table, the stork thought that the soup looked very tasty indeed.

With her napkin wrapped tidily round her slender neck, the stork bent to taste the soup. Unfortunately the plates in which the fox had served the soup were very shallow. The poor stork, with her long pointed beak, could not manage to sup the delicious liquid properly. She tried again and again, turning her beak this way and that, but all she could manage to get was the tiniest drop at the end of her beak.

As the stork did not wish to be rude, she said nothing to the fox, but hoped that he might see that she was having difficulty and offer some help. But the fox did not seem to notice. He was too busy noisily lapping up his own soup.

Poor Stork was in despair. She was so hungry after her walk to the fox's house and now she couldn't eat her dinner! The fox paid her not the slightest bit of attention until he had finished the last drop of his own soup. Only then did he notice that the stork's plate was still almost full.

"Miss Stork, I see you have a very small appetite, for you have hardly touched your soup! Or perhaps you didn't like it very much?"

The stork opened her beak to explain, but the fox didn't wait for an answer.

"Never mind," he said, "I'm hungry enough for two!"

Before the Stork could protest, he reached over, grabbed her plate, and gobbled up all of her lovely soup.

The stork was astonished that the fox could be so rude and thoughtless. She began to wonder if he had given her a shallow plate on purpose, just to make her feel awkward. However, she was determined not to let him see just how upset she was. Taking a deep breath, she turned to the fox and said calmly— "Thank you for a very nice evening. I would very much like to repay your kindness. Would you like to come and have dinner with me at my house next week?"

The fox licked the last drops of soup from round his mouth and smiled.

"I would be delighted to come, thank you. I shall look forward to it, Miss Stork."

The stork then politely bade him goodbye and left.

The following week, just as had been arranged, the fox prepared himself for his dinner with the stork. With his fur carefully licked clean, he strode along the path to the stork's house feeling very cheerful. As he got nearer the stork's house the fox sniffed the air thoughtfully. There was a wonderful, delicious smell wafting through the stork's open kitchen window.

"That must be my dinner," thought the fox with delight. "It smells as if I am going to be treated to something very special indeed!"

He bounded up the steps and rang the doorbell.

The stork greeted the fox with a gracious smile and led him into her cosy house.

"It is nice to see you again Mr Fox," she said. "Dinner will be ready in a moment or two. Please take a seat."

"I'm looking forward to it very much Miss Stork," said the fox greedily. "That walk has given me quite an appetite, and there is a very tasty smell coming from your kitchen."

"Just a simple stew, Mr Fox," replied the stork quietly. "If you'll excuse me, I'll just go to the kitchen and dish it up."

A few moments later, the stork returned from the kitchen carrying two tall, long-necked flagons, which she placed on the table.

"Here we are Mr Fox, dinner is served," she said.

The fox looked at the flagons. Surely he wasn't to eat from one of these things? Or perhaps he would be given a plate to pour the contents of the flagon into? The stork pretended not to see how puzzled the fox was.

"Please start," she said politely, "and enjoy your meal."

Then she gave a little smile, dipped her long beak right down into her flagon, and began to eat.

The fox picked up his own flagon and looked at it. The stork carried on eating. The fox pushed his nose into the neck of the flagon. His nose got stuck halfway down, tantalisingly out of reach of the fragrant stew in the bottom of the flagon. The stork was just about finished her own meal when at last she looked up the fox.

"Is something the matter, Mr Fox?" she smiled.

The fox pulled the flagon from his aching nose with a 'pop!' He looked very embarrassed.

"I'm sorry Miss Stork," he said "but I can't eat it this way!"

"Dear me, what a pity," said the stork. "I shall just have to eat your stew for you. Pass me your flagon will you, please?"

The fox was most indignant. He stood up and spoke angrily to the stork.

"I think, Miss Stork," he said, "that you are treating me both rudely and unkindly. This is poor hospitality indeed, serving me a meal that I cannot reach to eat!"

The stork looked at the fox calmly.

"Perhaps that is so, Mr Fox. But you were the one who set me the example when I came to your house for dinner last week. You cannot complain to me for doing as you did."

The stork was smiling as the fox left. He had learned his lesson.